31/5/21

With love.

Julie x

CONTENTS

INTRODUCTION

A MESSAGE FROM ME to YOU

I hope you like what lies within,
As I found quite amusing,
The words I wrote upon the page,
Will never be confusing.

You see, I have a simple mind,
And can be very childish,
I never really have grown up,
But strive to be so stylish.

I always like to have a laugh,
I hope that you'll agree,
The words I've wrote within the book,
Are written for you and me.

If I've put a smile upon your face,
With words that took the Mick,
And silly illustrations too,
Then I know they've done the trick!

This book is sponsored by:

ZMS Consulting & Coaching
Zlatica M. Stubbs, MA, PCC, MKcS

With Thanks

Ed Christiano and Deeperblue for the Cover Arrangement

DEAR READERS

In this book I have included a little friend of mine in each illustration, can you spot it?

I love this little friend of mine,
I've grown to love it well,
It likes to walk around at night,
What tales that it could tell.
Of all which sleep in slumberland,
The noises we each make,
When snoring with one's mouth agape,
Until we all awake.
I love this little friend of mine,
But many they will not,
If only they could grow to love,
Then they won't need to swat.
I love this little friend of mine,
So next time when you see,
This little friend I love a lot,
Please will you leave it be.

LITTLE BUMBLE BEE

I am a little bumble bee,
I flit from flower to flower,
I flit along with buzzing song,
Armed with a little power.

A power I hold within my sting,
It sits there on my bottom,
A sting I hope I never use,
As I will be begotten!

For I am really so laid back,
It's for my sole protection,
Leave me alone to pollinate,
I'm not one that boasts perfection.

People run when I buzz by,
But I really don't care less,
That you are there, just leave me be,
I could do without the stress!

I'm just a little bumble bee,
I flit from flower to flower,
I flit along with buzzing song,
To pass away the hour.

J. E. Graven

THIS WORM

Whist out in the garden digging one day,

Up popped a worm coming out to play.

I didn't find it funny as it made me jump,

Making one fall over with an almighty thump.

That worm didn't bother as it wiggled away,

But me looking muddy so be as it may.

I pulled myself up and brushed myself down,

I then got this worm that came up from the ground.

I picked it up as it wiggled and squirmed,

And then over the fence went that horrible worm.

I heard a little splash as their pond it did land,

Was it the end of that worm that came up from the ground?

J. E. Craven

CATERPILLAR

I have a little caterpillar
I've named her greedy May,
I have her in a jam jar,
And I feed her every day.

She moves around the jam jar,
Feeding as she goes,
She's only small, she can't get far,
In spite her many toes.

It won't be long just wait and see,
I'll lose my greedy May,
For she will cease too ever be,
As no longer will she stay.

She went to sleep cocooned so tight,
Until that magic time,
When May would come prepared for flight,
And burst forth no longer mine.

From caterpillar to cabbage white,
May's now a butterfly,
And off she set with all her might,
In flight up to the sky.

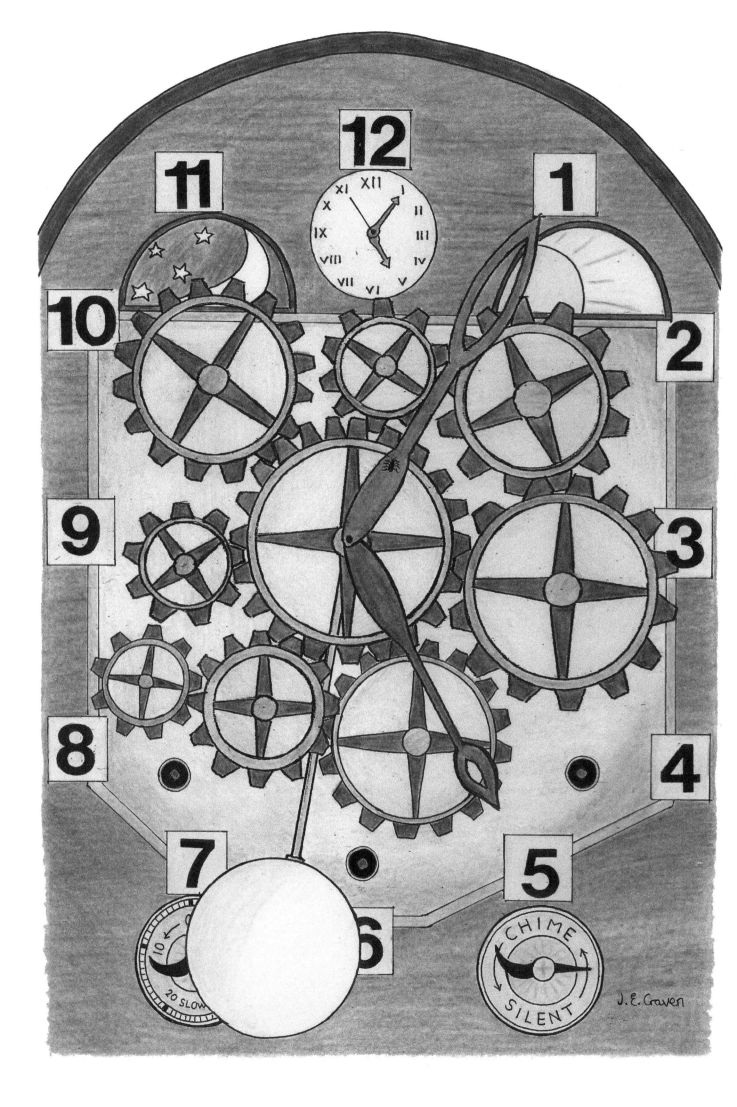

TICK TOCK CLOCK

Have you ever stopped and thought?
About the time old tick tock clock,
Of cogs and wheels and wheels and cogs,
Pieced together as they interlock.
Her hand is moved per minute,
As the minutes turn to hours,
Tick tock tick tock,
Sixty minutes to the hour.

Time is very cleaver,
Our lives are ruled upon it,
From the rising of the sun,
And the turning of the tide,
The moon which shines above us,
And the stars up in the sky,
The old tick tock clock,
Of which we always must abide.

The hours turn into days
And then comes forth the months,
The time flies by without us,
Really knowing what's to come,
But that old tick tock clock,
Of which we must succumb,
Tick tock tick tock,
Time stands still for not one man.

The months turn into years
We age our bodies growing,
Older as the tick tock clock,
Never stops but keeps on going,
As the sun will always rise,
And the tides will keep on turning,
Our lives fly fast but one thing's sure,
We will always keep on yearning.

For all those wasted years,
Now our time is nearly done,
From being born to getting old,
It hasn't all been fun.
But I know there's one sure thing,
Which you will always see,
And that's the old tick tock clock,
As this clock will always be.

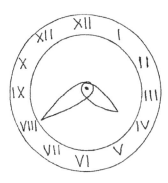

TOILET

If only toilets had a voice,
What tales that they could tell,
Of all which sits upon this throne,
That dangle down the well.

There's those who sit to have a poo,
Who push but only gas,
Comes forth with gust, a smell so foul,
Straight from one's big round ass.

It isn't funny when those who've been,
To dine and eaten curry,
For sure enough the very next day,
The loo now they must hurry.

They sit upon the loo with haste,
Not long before it comes,
The poo which pebble dashes 'round,
The basin, how it hums.

When constipation troubles come,
A lot to comprehend,
Why one's poo when pushed on through,
Will go and block the bend.

When cheeks a spread and one must guess,
What parcels are to come?
From soft to hard or rabbit bobs,
We wish that we could run.

We sigh with glee when only pee,
Is splashed around the pot,
Until next time we'll have to see,
Might be the ruddy lot!

KNICKERS

The sun is shining brightly, with a tiny little breeze,
I think I'll go a walking and flash my pretty knees.
I'll wear this little number; the one that's short and cute,
Which turns the heads of men in cars, as they give a little toot.

So off I set to wonder, to stretch my lanky legs,
And it wasn't long before, I started to turn heads.
A man gave out a whistle and his horn he then did press,
When along came a wind and lifted up my dress.

The car then hit a lamppost, as I turned and looked in ponder,
Had he never ever seen a pair of knickers I did wonder.
It wasn't until later, as off home I then did run,
And found out to my amazement, I'd forgot to put them on.

DEAR OLD SANTA

When Santa came down the chimney,
He had the surprise of his life,
He never imagined his stomach,
Had grown bigger than that of his wife.
He got wedged there right in the middle,
And came out in a sweat as he knew,
The more that he struggled and wiggled,
The stomach of his only grew.
It swelled a little bit bigger,
As he shouted to Rudolf to come,
Throw down those reins please hurry,
When I tell you get ready to run.
Dear Rudolf set off with a jolt,
And Santa shot out like a cork,
He landed on top of his carriage,
In shock was unable to talk.
He sat there for just a few minutes,
Before he got hold of his sack,
He had to deliver the presents,
Before he made his way back.
This time he went through the window,
And placed presents all under the tree,
No chimneys in future for Santa,
Relieved his Rudolf had pulled him free.
It had to be all of those mince pies,
Which Santa enjoyed every year,
He'll just have to go on strict diet,
So, the chimneys he'll go without fear.
The following year dear old Santa,
Had shed an almighty two stone,
He slipped down the chimneys no trouble,
Then shattered he headed for home.

TEETH

My teeth were clean my teeth were
bright,
I brushed them twice a day,
The toothpaste which I always used,
Was there to stop decay.

But when a little older,
My teeth I did neglect,
I never brushed them twice a day,
It fills me with regret.

As now I'm old and wrinkly.
No toothpaste do I choose,
Only that old denture stuff,
Is what I have to use.

And as I lie there in my bed,
Hearing that fizzle overhead,
I only wish, I had been,
More careful with my teeth!

WASP

A wasp had blooming stung me,
There upon my bum,
It hurts a lot there on my bot,
As I run home to mum.

She said, "Come here I'll have a look",
As I dropped down my kecks,
Bare bum revealed for mum to see,
She then put on her specks.

"Oh dear", said she, when closer looked,
"I see the sting so clearly,
I'll have to try and pull it out",
And tried alas, did nearly.

Pull out that sting but couldn't grip,
With tweezers mum did try,
Failing this she'll have to suck,
One really can't be shy.

Mum's lips locked on to my poor bum,
And she sucked until this sting,
Come forth at last but my poor mum,
Swallowed the blessed thing.

I pulled up trolleys to cover ass,
No sting in painful bum,
Then out to play again once more,
Thank goodness for my dear mum.

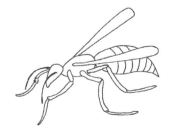

FIGHT 1972

There's going to be a fight tonight,
Outside school out of sight,
Where no grown-ups will interfere,
And come along to box an ear,
Or two as if by right.
 They're going to wait for Tiny Tim,
 So, Johnny Green can batter him,
 They said he'd done it once before,
 And gave him one right on the nose,
 Which busted it right open.
  Bad Johnny Green hit him again,
  As blood poured out of his squashed snout,
  And made it look unreal,
  So, Johnny Green gave him another,
  As Tiny Tim ran home to mother to tell of his ordeal.
   His mother yelled out, "Look at your snout,
   You'll never get another,
   Let's clean it up and have a look,
   MY GOD, GOOD GRIEF, OH BROTHER!
    From that day on it has been said,
    This naughty Johnny Green,
    Has had it in for Tiny Tim,
    For his informing over him,
    About him being mean!
     So, after school this very day,
     He waits to plant another,
     But who was there not Tiny Tim,
     He'd only brought his mother.
      Who marched him off with ear in hand,
      Straight down to see Headmaster,
      It can now be said big Johnny Green,
      Has the reddest ass here after!

J. E. Craven

THE DREADED FLEA

Have you ever had this annoying itch?
The more you scratch the more you twitch.
It seems to move in another place,
When up pops a lump, now one has to face.

The thought of a flea might be in one's clothes,
How do I catch it? Heaven only knows.
It's from the garden as the cat lay basking,
It crept in her fur cunningly masking.

She then came inside and snuggled all up,
There on my clothes which was nicely piled-up.
So now I've been given a few little bites,
As I take off my clothes to see where it hides.

It's like trying to find, needle in haystack,
As flea is illusive, impossible to track.
So, clothes are then covered in plenty of spray,
Goodbye and good riddance and hip hip hurray!

J.E. Craven

BEAUTIFUL EARTH

Don't take for granted in all which you see,

The Earth is a beauty forever to be.

Take care of this precious and wonderful gem,

To destroy and destruct, is the final Amen.

Take time, take in all, Earth's glory, you'll see,

A beautiful creation for you and for me.

From the birds and the bees to the flowers and trees,

To the fish and the whales, it all never fails.

To amaze you and me all that walks on this land,

In the forests and desserts and beaches of sand.

We should all join together and hold hand in hand,

To save all which dwells on this incredible land.

The skies will get angry the rivers burst banks,

The tides will start rising and then who will we thank.

Not God but mankind are the ones that's to blame,

Stand up and be counted put heads down in shame,

Save all the birds, bees, flowers and trees,

The fish and the whales so it all never fails.

The forests and desserts and beaches of sand,

And all that dwells on this incredible land.

For all mankind should walk hand in hand,

So, we all start to save this incredible land.

SCRUMMY FOOD

Every time I try to diet, I end up eating more,

I start off being really good, it then becomes a bore!

A diet's really not for me as I don't like much veg,

I seldom eat a lot of fruit it leaves me on the edge.

The edge of driving me insane as I love my food a lot,

All the food I shouldn't eat like burgers, chips, hotpot.

A cream cake I will not refuse and chocolate's very yummy,

A fresh cream trifles very nice as it slides into my tummy.

A crumpet laced with lots of butter and blueberry jam on toast,

I've put away many a pud but I'm not one to boast.

A coffee made with full fat milk with millionaire shortbread,

The things I know I shouldn't have; I should listen to my head.

As all the things I like the most are not good for my heart,

I'm going to have to try much harder and definitely have to start.

To start and eat a lot less fat and maybe eat more fish,

A yoghurt might go down ok as one can only wish.

To sum it up one can see, a bit of what you fancy,

Is not so bad when as a treat and should be fine and dandy.

THE FART

Has one ever thought about the fart which escapes out from one's bum?
The many different noises made, and the many farts that hum.
So, amusing often it can be, and equally embarrassing,
Depending on what's roundabout, and who you might be gassing.

Some farts do have a pungent smell, depending on what's eaten,
Hot and silent and most deadly, the ones which can't be beaten.
Some people say that they've passed wind, and some may say they've pumped,
Others may say they've had a fart, the rest may say they've trumped.

There're farts that play a little tune, which last a good few seconds,
And some come forth with a mighty blast, with another one that beckons.
The fart it is a funny thing, the different sounds it gives us,
Depending on the size of bum, and tightness of one's anus.

A fat ass gives a muffled sound; a tight ass gives a squeak,
A slack ass, who knows what's to come, and what lies up their creek.
When farts let rip in nudist camp, one hopes one is not near,
Just in case a wet one's brewed, that pebbles from one's rear.

Some people get disgusted, to hear one's fart let rip,
But I blow of when needed, as one's stomach would give the jip.
One could say it's a slight explosion, from one's ass where gas breaks free,
When said and done it's normal, so to hell what will be, will be.

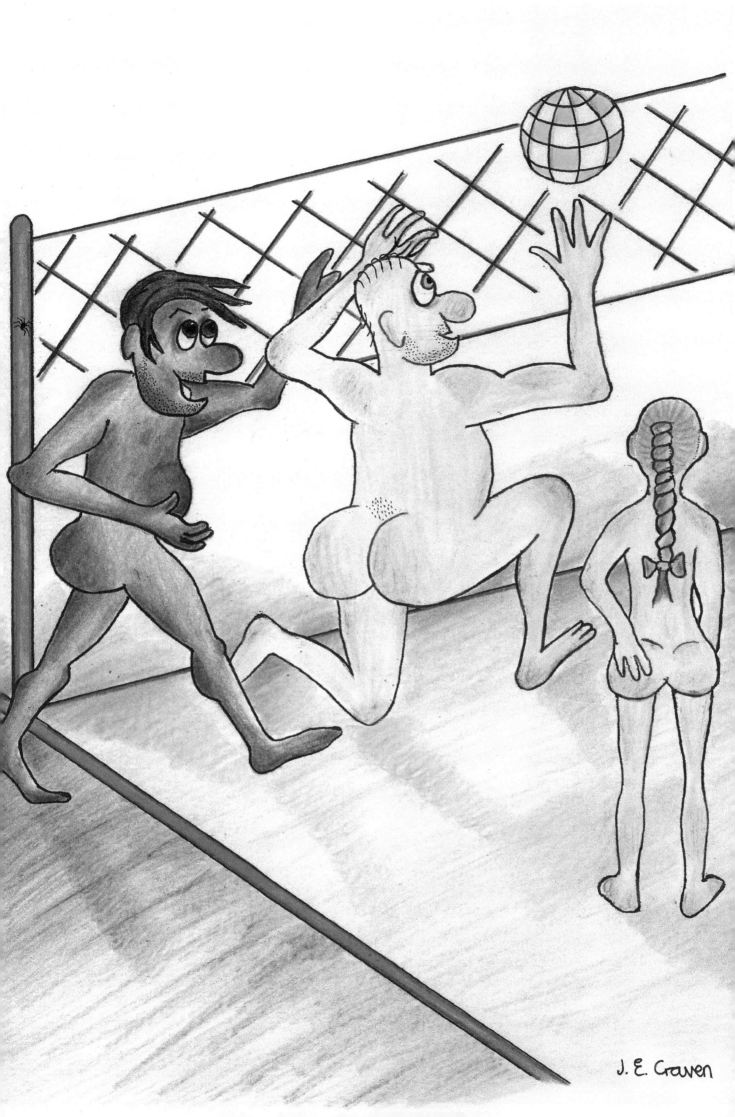

J. E. Craven

NUDIST CAMP

How funny is the nudist camp?
With many shapes and sizes,
There's lots of different dangly bits,
One can see whose bums the widest.

The men they stroll their bits on show,
Embarrassment not in it,
Some big, some small, some fat, some thin,
With a wig of hair to fit.

Some women proud of what they've got,
With breasts the size of melons,
While others not as much on top,
Resembling some lemons.

The older ladies' breasts gone south,
As age has taken hold,
But still, they walk with pride and stance,
But I think them very bold.

It's fun to watch the volleyball,
No need for imagination,
Their every private bit on show,
Looked ready for separation.

They flopped and swayed, wiggled and bounced,
And then to top it all,
A man bent down to pick up ball,
Why did he have to sprawl?

His legs apart and ass in air,
All hung down there in full,
For what was dangling there between,
Just looked like farmer's bull.

A nudist camp is not for me,
Not one to bare it all,
My private bits are only viewed,
By spouse and Doctor on call!

J. E. Graven

PEOPLE

One likes to frequent coffee shops,
And watch the world pass by,
What delights there is to see,
With many a naked thigh.

    Thighs which are bigger than my waist
    All naked to the top,
    Imagination next to none,
    Which made many a man's eyes pop.

        How times have changed from bygone years,
        Where all was covered up,
        Not now as all revealed on show,
        With many a DD cup.

            These breasts they wobble and bounce along,
            All bulging and looking like jelly,
            But not as bad as some cropped tops,
            That exhibit many a fat belly.

                The bellies jiggle with every step took,
                Some navel piercings done,
                As some pass by, oh my oh my,
                One's faced with an almighty bum.

            A bum that's squeezed in mini skirt,
            How did one get it on?
            One hopes they never have to bend,
            As one would block the sun.

        There are better clothes to buy that suits,
        One's different body shape,
        So, cover up to look real good,
        Don't leave it all to gape.

We're all unique and beautiful,
Just wear what suits you best,
Be proud of who you really are,
And strive to be best dressed!

LEPRECHAUN

I am a little Leprechaun; my home is in a boot,

I live with all my siblings, and life is such a hoot.

I say it with such sarcasm, as life is one long squabble,

As our boot is small and tightly packed, but at least it's not a hovel,

We have to all sleep top to toe, with smelly feet to wrestle,

And while asleep to top it all, a fart or two would whistle,

Snoring one cannot escape, not easy to dismiss,

A nudge or two will have to do, to put a stop to this.

Our mum she loves us dearly, her wee little leprechauns,

We run her ragged and often do, but we're loved from dawn 'till dawn!

Our boot has many an eyelet, as windows which perfectly fit,

Our neighbours they think we are nosey, so stuff them the miserable gits!

Our garden it gives us our freedom, to play as all leprechauns do,

We hide and seek until nature calls, where a bush is our God sent loo.

I am a little leprechaun; my home is in a boot,

I live with all my siblings, but life is NOT a hoot.

YIPPEE SNOW

Snow is falling from the sky; children wait for it to stick.

They throw snowballs at passers-by, those naughty kids they trick.

"Go get your sledge," says George to Bob, as Bob now asks his mum,

Then Bob tells Sue who then tells Rob, then off to have some fun.

Wheeee screams Bob while sledging down, with George and Rob behind.

Poor Sue falls off, begins to frown, but Bob's a hill to climb.

They played for hours such fun was had, the snow it did the trick.

All love to sledge it makes them glad, but time would fly so quick.

Until next day and snow anew, they sledge upon that hill,

George and Bob with Rob and Sue, with lots of time to kill.

But sadly, all good things must end, the snow began to melt,

The wonderful sight of winter white, but always so heartfelt.

TROUBLE

There is a naughty little boy,
His middle name is trouble,
The pranks which normal boys will do,
You most certainly will double.

When daddy longlegs take to flight,
   And trouble is about,
   He starts to catch them one by one,
   Their legs he will cast out.

A catapult he likes to use,
   In comic he got free,
Those little stones go hurtling by,
   At birds he does with glee.

On a beaut-i-ful warm day,
And sun beats down its rays,
A magnifying glass he has,
He burns those bugs for days.

He likes to capture butterflies,
   Different species if he can,
   Then pin them to a board to see,
   If all does go to plan.

He has a dreaded chemistry set,
   Experiments he does,
A stink so foul set off in school,
   Which gives him such a buzz.

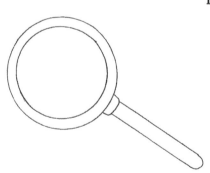

When trouble grows into a man,
And reflects on creature's past,
The pain instilled upon them all,
Remorse he'll feel at last!

BEDTIME

It's time for bed for sister and I,
It's time to say goodnight,
We always say, "Hope you sleep tight,
Don't let the bedbugs bite."

For me it's time to have some fun,
As my sister tries to sleep,
I slowly slip out of my bed,
As I try my best to creep,

I carefully creep around the bed,
And in my sister's ear I do,
Blast out with gust which is so funny,
An almighty sounding BOO!

She darted underneath the sheets,
And screamed, "That wasn't funny!
I'll have to go and sit on loo,
You've upset my blooming tummy!"

When back in bed with sleepy head,
We sing a song or two,
Then off to sleep there's not a peep,
'Till morning starts anew.

40

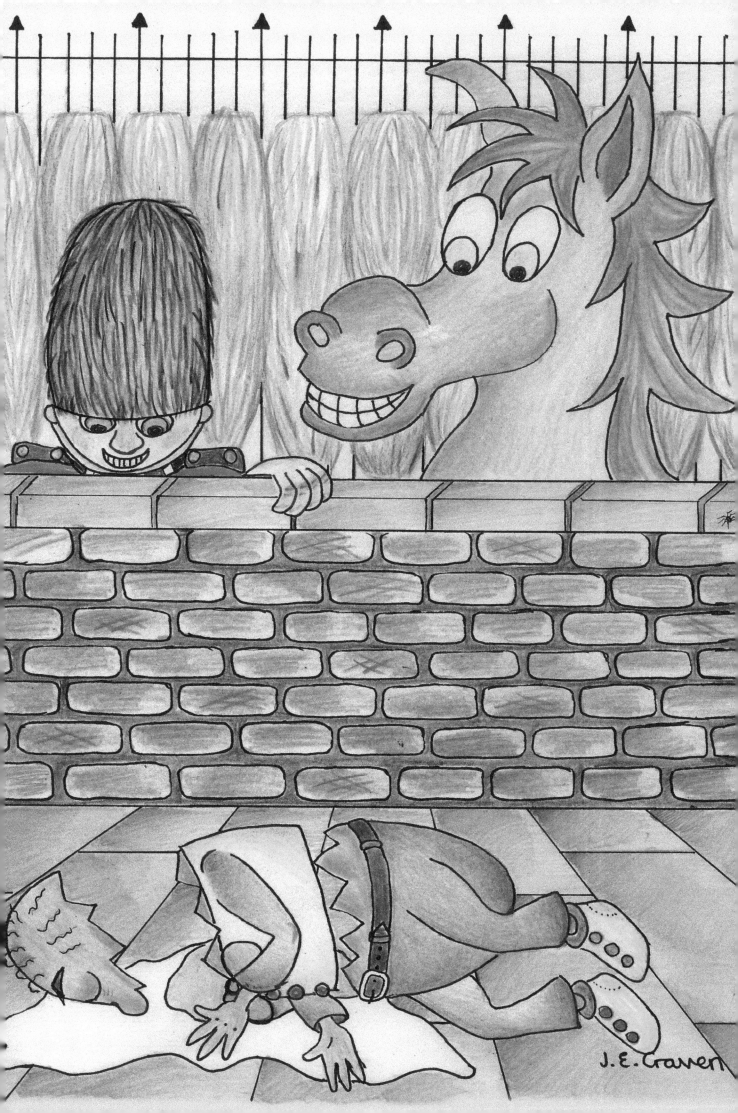

HUMPTY'S ACTUAL DEMISE

There is an egg that's spoken in rhyme,
His name is Humpty Dumpty,
He came about from mother hen,
Just after rumpy pumpy.

How Humpty Dumpty came about,
To sit upon this wall,
It baffles one to how he did,
As he wasn't very tall!

Were all those Queen's horses,
And all those Queen's men,
Which put poor Humpty Dumpty,
On the wall there and then!

They'd come up with a plan,
About Humpty's demise,
A Royal conspiracy,
Poor Humpty's to die!

The next thing you knew,
Poor Humpty was pushed,
Was those horsemen and Queen's men,
For it all had been hushed!

Humpty Dumpty cracked open,
And out popped his brain,
To mend him they couldn't,
They tried but in vain!

And from that day on,
Humpty Dumpty made fame,
Was from death he's remembered,
It was such a shame!

J. E. Craven

SEAGULLS!!!

I live at the seaside fresh air gentle breeze,

Watch the waves and white horses, paddle up to my knees.

I walk down the coastline with sand between toes,

With starfish and seashells to see as one goes,

Then along came the seagulls, my peace is then shattered,

They flew overhead; oh my God I'd been splattered!

It ran down my head, then dripped on my face,

There were splats on my t-shirt; I was in the wrong place!

It smelt rather putrid; it made me feel sick,

It was just as if they had been taking the Mick!

I searched in my pocket, a tissue I found,

As I wiped off the bird poo, that terrible mound!

It sounded as if they were laughing at me,

With their loud gull cry, not one, two but three!

I love where I live, putting seagull's aside,

It's a wonderful haven, my beautiful seaside!

CHRISTMAS

The trees are bare, no leaves to fall,

Autumn took them, one and all.

I'm sure the birds that I could see,

Would surely want to agree,

Is when the winter came in sight,

The snow would come the warmth would go,

And all the children which we knew,

Would go to Santa at the store,

To tell him what they wanted when,

The 25th of December came.

When the night of excitement came,

All was calm all was peaceful.

Children sleeping in their beds,

Gave little sighs as if to say,

Is it time, time to see,

All that Santa's brought for me?

Not one did stir not one did peep,

In case Santa was caught on the creep,

I'm sure all others would agree,

They love their Christmas as much as me!

THREADWORMS!!!

Threadworms, threadworms, threadworms galore,

My botty is a tickling; I think I'm getting more!

They start to wiggle all about, as I squeeze my botty tight,

The threadworms like to lay their eggs, when I'm fast asleep at night!

They slip outside my botty, to get their duty done,

But the tickling is persistent, so I go to scratch my bum!

Eggs get stuck right up my nails, without my even knowing,

And because they're microscopic, there's nothing which is showing!

So, when getting out of bed, and downstairs I then do trot,

My hands I am supposed to wash, but I just clean forgot!

I went and ate my breakfast, and then passed onto my toast,

Those little eggs from up my nails, under my unsuspecting nose!

So now all my breakfast's eaten, and everything's digested,

I have to now inform you; I've just been re-infested!

So, if ever you get threadworms, a chemist you must see,

And make sure you wash and scrub your nails,

so you'll be threadworm free!!!

JOURNEY

I arose at the crack of dawn,
Said goodbye, the morning anew,
Went for my bike and peddled at speed,
Past the park across the town,
On to the countryside.

Up the hill and down the dale,
Pedalled my way through wooded glades,
Over the bridge of a babbling brook,
Noticed the cows who stood and gazed,
As I pedalled on my way.

The sun it shone no clouds to see,
Just a gentle breeze to cool the face,
As the flowers swayed their colours mingled,
Magnificent, a blanket spread,
Free in abundance stood.

Those birds sing sweet as butterflies dance,
The day is theirs amongst buttercups,
Clover, bluebells, tall grasses sway,
Trees whispering as they stood,
What beauty the wilderness looks!

I rode until the sun went down,
The day near close and night owl hoot,
I pedalled back past babbling brook,
Sped my way through wooded glade,
Up dale, downhill, back home from the countryside.

GNOME

I am a little happy gnome,
And love my garden dearly!
I sit beside a lily pond,
And watch the fish so clearly.

I sit and watch the fish swim by,
How calming it can be,
And sometimes frogs on lily pad,
Will croak across at me.

I have a little girlfriend gnome,
Which I am very fond of,
One day I hope she's placed by me,
Forever and thereof.

I watch the birds to pass the time,
They squabble over tit bits,
They hop around across the ground,
The Goldfinch, Blackbird, Blue tit.

There's many a worm that's crossed my path,
Along with slugs and earwigs,
They move along and say hello,
When master comes and digs.

Today must be my lucky day,
I now have what I wished for,
My girlfriend gnome sits next to me,
From now and ever more!

52

NED

One hears the sound of Ned's big shoes, clipperty clop, clipperty clop,
The bridal way is his to cruise, clipperty clop, clipperty clop.

When who should he meet but billy bunny, hopperty hop, hopperty hop,
"You nearly trod on me, not very funny!" hopperty hop, hopperty hop.

Ned bids good day and off he trots, clipperty clop, clipperty clop,
When up in the distance he hears some shots, clipperty clop, clipperty clop,

He sees old Ben the farmer's dog, he's barking mad, barking mad,
Who warns of hunters down in't bog, he's barking mad, barking mad.

He'll have to see if old deer's safe, clipperty clop, clipperty clop,
No time to lose he'll have to race, clipperty clop, clipperty clop.

He spies old deer behind a bush, quivering wreck, quivering wreck,
So still is deer, she needs to hush, quivering wreck, quivering wreck.

Ned leaves her safe as off he trots, clipperty clop, clipperty clop,
Another shot as birdie flops, clipperty clop, clipperty clop.

Ned feels so sad as birdie's dead, birdie's dead, birdie's dead.
He comes to a halt and bows his head, birdie's dead, birdie's dead.

Ned slumps away with heavy heart, clip clop, clip clop,
So sad is he as birdie parts, clip clop clip..................!

MY BLINKING HAT

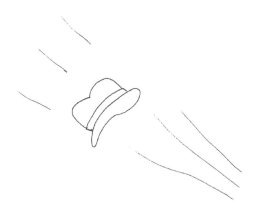

Whilst walking in the park one day,
A hat I had to don,
The wind was so ferocious,
Then my hat blew off and gone.
It blew along the footpath,
And up into the air,
I ran to try and catch my hat,
One could only feel despair!
It flew across a park bench,
A passer bye gave out a smile,
I gasped as it was blown some more,
For just a little while.
I hurried on to catch it up,
I could see it just ahead,
My hat a little worse for wear,
To lose it I did dread!

My hat was there just insight,
As I start to pick up pace,
It got stuck just by a litter bin,
I was surely in a race!
A race to catch my blinking hat,
It hadn't been much fun!
Nearly there, a few more runs,
Not knowing what's to come!
A lady bent to pick it up,
I shouted, "Hoy that's mine!"
I hurried up a little more,
But got there out of time!
She looked at my bedraggled hat,
And placed it in that bin,
If only I had held my hat,
Right from the very beginning'!!!

J. E. Craven

VISITORS

There's a knock at the door, who can it be?
I'll have to get up to go look and see!
I walk down the hall and through frosted glass,
See two figures stood waiting, then suddenly gasp!

Please don't let it be those annoying few,
Who arrive in pairs, if one only knew!
Can you guess who they are, you've probably had,
A few on your doorstep, to drive you mad!

One tries to say nicely, no thank you not now,
And would stop them returning, if one only knew how!
I don't understand why they keep on persisting,
To pester the public when we keep on resisting!

It's a pity they've nothing else better to do,
Than to pour their own views on to me and to you!
There's a knock at the door, they've not gone away,
As I peep round the curtain to see why they stay.

Thank goodness for that, it's not them at all,
It's just mum and dad who've decided to call.
So, take heed all you pairs, the next time you call,
When refused we DO mean, you're NOT wanted at all!!

SPITTING

I don't know why it is today,
People spit upon the floor!
They have to spit along the way,
Or any place they go!

I have to walk along and look,
The footpath there to see,
To guarantee I'm not about,
And have one stick on me!

I'm baffled as to why one spits,
It makes me feel resent,
Does one think it makes one bigger?
In front of others present!

Do parents know of their kids' doings?
Or unconcerned to see,
What their kids do in front of others,
And the germs which there might be!

One is Tuberculosis,
And there are viruses galore,
The germs that's spread to you and me,
Please stop so it's no more!

So, hear all you people old,
The ones who cough and spit,
It's time that you now showed the kids,
Not to spit but swallow it!!!

GETTING UP

The alarm goes off, "Get out of bed",
I shout to all the others,
"We can't be late its school today,
Sally go and wake your brothers."

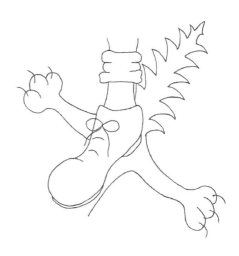

"Brush your teeth, wash your face,
Go back and flush that chain,
Mind the cat, whoops too late,
You've stepped on him again!"

I'm not surprised he does insist,
On wrapping round, one's legs
"Unlock the door and let him out,
Before we break our necks"!

It's breakfast time I'm coping fine,
I always do my best,
To try and make each different food,
Which each of them request.

"Sit down grub up", I say at last,
"How are we fixed for time"?
"Okay", they said," We're not too late,
We'll still get there for nine",

So, when at last they'd all ate up,
I kissed them all farewell,
"Make sure you hurry, don't dilly dally,
Or else you'll miss the bell"!

I step inside and shut the door,
Thank goodness breakfast's
done,
You'll never know how hard it is,
To be a model mum!!!

DOGGY POO

It's the same old story; I've said it before,
Watch out for that dog poo, I can't stand it anymore!

It's the children you see going out to play,
All happy and excited, they're such an easy prey!

They play on the grass a game of football or two,
While lurking in the distance is a lump of poo!

I saw the doggy do it, it was hers next door,
I'll go and tell dog warden if she leaves once more!

She lets it off its lead, 'till its business is done,
Then left upon the field to play and have a little fun!

It wasn't long before I caught sight of my son,
Who'd tripped and found he'd only put his hand in some!

I hate to see dog owners, who couldn't care less,
Those unsuspecting children come and fall in the mess!

They should be made responsible for their doggy's number
two's,
And fined a lot of money if they don't clean up their poo's!

I'm sure I'd be reported if I let my children poo,
There upon the grass outside, just like their doggy's do!!!

MY PUSSY CAT

I have a little pussy cat I love with all my heart,
She snuggles up and loves me back, for we shall never part.
She loves to watch the birds fly past, while looking through the window,
Those birds she'll dream when fast asleep, her head upon my pillow.

She has her crazy moments, darting here and there,
She even runs up on my wall, as I cry out in despair!
"Get down you naughty little puss, my wallpapers just ripped!
It isn't funny it costs me money to try and get it fixed"!

It's best when Christmas comes around, the tree it looks so fine,
I'm sure she thinks those balls upon, this tree is hers not mine.
She starts to bat them one by one until they all fall off,
Then chases them around the room, but the chocolate ones I scoff!

When summer's here the sun so hot, a window I would open,
Then in pops fly, annoying buzz, my pussy cat's awoken,
My cat will chase the fly around, with all that she can muster,
Is not my cat that gets the fly but is my blooming duster!

I love my little pussy cat, I love with all my heart,
One day when she is old and grey, her time on earth will part.
For its Gods will to take us all, for when our time is done,
My cat will chase those flies and balls, in heaven having fun.

I LOVE MY CAT!!!

SCHOOL

What a day I'll have at school, a teacher's what I am,
It's only nine the day is mine, they call me Mr. Sam.

The day unfolds to what it holds; we mustn't make a fuss,
We just have to go with the flow; it's always to be thus.

There's always one which has to be, a clown for all to see,
One acts the fool, oh what a tool, and deffo off their tree!

If only one could understand, that education matters,
You need your maths and English too, so life won't end in
tatters.

We teachers try to understand, what makes the children tick,
As some are bright, they'll all take flight, they never take the Mick!

If only all the children see, the importance of it all,
And study hard so they'll go far, so they will never fall.

Their futures written in the sand, the rest is up to them,
We teachers work, it is a perk, when they get ten from ten.

Then one grows up and strives to be, and hopes that very soon,
That life is good with happy years, no place of doom and gloom!

The moral is as plain to see, work hard so you can get,
And what you seek in life to be, your wishes shall be met!

68

BLACKBIRD

I wake up in the morning,

To the song the blackbird sings,

How beautiful to hear this sound,

And all its goodness brings.

He sits so proud upon the branch,

And holds his head up high,

His little beak he opens wide,

And a melody lets fly.

He is a plain self-coloured bird,

Jet black is all he wears,

But what a voice, those tuneful notes,

Black feathers, well, who cares?

The morning song of this dear bird,

Brings forth the day to come,

I rise and shine the day is mine,

I've work that must be done.

Until again now work has finished,

This bird before his flight,

He sings his song; it's time for bed,

Good night, God bless, sleep tight.

WASTE!!!

As I go and put out my dustbin,
   And the bin man's cart draws near,
      To empty all that's put within,
         Which smells in the atmosphere.

      A peg is needed upon my nose,
         As I whiff this pungent smell,
            Which once was laid there on my plate,
               For one should really dwell.

         As I add up the wasted cost,
            Of all that's put within,
               My old grey bin, each day I must,
                  Be shocked, oh what a sin!

         One can't begin to weigh the amount,
            From each and every one of us,
               When the shameful waste of all that food,
                  To feed the poor, would be a plus!

            So, when next time you fill your plate,
               Let it be just for your belly,
                  And NOT just destined for your bin,
                     Which ends up rotten and smelly!

WORK

I arise at four in the morning,
To start at 6am,
An early shift is what I do,
Then home in time for ten.
A cleaner is my title role,
A job, it's not for many,
There isn't a lot that can be got,
To be up at four, if any.
I love my job and all its lot,
Good exercise I get,
One moves a lot and never stops,
Burn calories, I bet!
There are a few, I could mention two,
Who thinks it is beneath them,
To use a cloth and dolly mop,
Not me, it's my little gem!
As I get paid to exercise,
And don't need the local gym,
I'm a fitter, energised, rounded gran,
But will never be skinny and thin!

BROTHER

My brother had two budgerigars,
Their names were Mork and Mindy,
We laughed when told of their two names,
But was better than Paul and Sindy.

He bought them toys and mirrors too,
To play with all day long,
Mork chirped away, was on top note,
Was little Morks loud song.

Sometimes they'd squabble, peck and flap,
Which he didn't find amusing,
As he loved his tele and couldn't hear,
So, the plot was quite confusing.

He'd throw a tiny little thing,
To stop them in their stride,
But in their cage, there wasn't room,
For them to go and hide.

It wasn't long when my dear brother,
Lost faith in Mork and Mindy,
Where Mork now sits with my dear mother,
At peace with his dear Mindy.

FESTIVITY

Christmas comes but once a year,
And costs a pretty penny,
There are Christmas cards and presents too,
With an awful lot of booze?
We'll stuff the bird and cook the pud,
Then eat and pack our bellies,
Sitting there fit to burst,
We then switch on the tele.

The kids run riot, the cat's berserk,
And the dog's chewed dads' new slippers,
The Christmas tree get knocked about,
While balls fall off and lights get broke,
And dad begins to lose his cool,
As he slowly rises to the floor,
"Shut up, sit down, think of your gran,
She's listening to Queen Speech"!

We pull our crackers then have some cake,
And play a game or two,
We laugh, we cry, we reminisce,
While the kids bat their balloons,
And as the day draws near to close,
And ready for our beds,
We lift our glasses and merrily toast,
Good health for all next year!!!

LONELINESS

As lonely as the loneliest,
He walks alone through new cropped
fields,
With thoughts so free.
Each silk thread hair blows furiously,
In winds which cry through old, barked
trees,
They're alone, alone so free.

No thoughts to mingle with curious
people,
All programmed, all different, individual
theories,
He journeys alone with nature
uncultured,
Flowers untouched, abundance in
colour,
A blanket laid out, magnificent
splendour,
He's alone, alone so free.

MELLY

There was an old dog called Melly,

Who fell down the stairs on his belly,

When Melly got up,

His belly got stuck,

And his legs had all turned to jelly.

BIRD

There was a young bird from Belize,

Who blew off a branch in the breeze,

He started to flap,

Did a big crap,

Then fluttered back up in the trees.

ROBIN

There up sat Cock Robin on roof,

Who was looking all smug and aloof,

When down dropped old Sparrow,

Shot dead by his arrow,

Was Cock Robin this time said in truth.

SNOT GOBBLERS

Why are fingers made to fit?
So perfect up one's nose,
Those little fingers poke about,
To pick those little crows.

One picks and prods until one comes,
And then it's rolled about,
This green and crusty little snot,
Right from one's tiny snout.

But there are some who like to place,
That snot into one's mush,
Who couldn't care if one had seen,
Not one to keep it hush.

So never mind, kids are kids,
Snot gobblers some become,
Just leave them be to eat away,
It's better to keep stumb!

I hope that you enjoyed within,

This book that I had written

And wish that you would kindly tell,

Your friends if you were smitten.

As I enjoyed the time I spent,

On planning all inside,

In trying to write it all in rhyme,

Of this I really tried.

For now, ones had a slight insight,

What might be coming next,

For in my second poem book,

The pictures and the text.

I hope you'll all now go and buy,

My second poem book,

When it's all done and out to buy,

So, you can have a look.

For now, it's time to say goodbye,

And thank you once again,

For all who's gone and bought this book,

Hope it wasn't all in vain.

Lightning Source UK
Milton Keynes UK
UKHW040926180920
370089UK00002BA/14/J

Lightning Source UK Ltd.
Milton Keynes UK
UKHW050033180621
385535UK00003B/2